for Odette

Written and illustrated by Lindsey Lonergan

This book belongs to

_____

The food that isn't safe for me is

_____

My swap bop first visited me on

_____

Did you know that some foods can make people sick? Sometimes it can hurt just from a lick!

Might be dairy, eggs, gluten,
shellfish or a nut.
They could hurt your tummy,
your head or your gut.

The good news is
when you're in this position,
you're assigned a BOP
who will help your condition!

A bop is a creature.
It's furry and small.
It loves to bounce
and roll in a ball!

But what it loves most
is the food you can't eat.
It'll gobble it up!
It loves a good treat.

In exchange for your food
it will make you a deal.
It will give you a trade
for a good meal.

Just leave it some food
that you can't eat
and it will swap you a prize.

Maybe food? Something else?
It's up to your bop.
It will be a surprise.

From a funfair,

a day trip

or from a play date.

Your bop will swap, it can hardly wait!

Just find a box
to make the swap.
You can decorate it
to get ready for your bop.

Put your food in the box
and leave that space.
Your bop will leave something
nice in its place.

It can never be seen
so don't try to peak!
When it's sure you're not looking
in it will sneak

It might wait for bedtime
when you're sleeping at last.
Or during the day.
You won't see, it's so fast!

Halloween is fun
for the spooky treats to snag.
Go trick-or-treating
and fill up your bag.

Box what you can't have.
Keep what you can.
The bop will then trade.
It knows the plan.

Christmas is the best!
When Santa comes a'knocking.
Festive treats all round,
maybe some in your stocking!

Hot chocolate, candy canes, gingerbread men,
whatever you're not allowed.
Just place them carefully in the box.
Your bop will be so proud!

Your bop adores special days
and any celebration!

Any time there is a chance
of a food donation.

If you're going somewhere
just let your bop know.
It will leave you food to take along
before it's time to go.

Sometimes you might miss out on a treat
but have no food to trade.

Just leave your bop a little note
and a swap will be made.

Not eating like other kids
might make you sad.
But your bop will be there so
you don't feel too bad.

You are special and strong.
Lucky is how you can feel.
Out of all the other kids,
who else has this fun deal?

Always remember when offered food
be careful and take care.
Ask a parent or teacher if it's ok.
It's great to be aware.

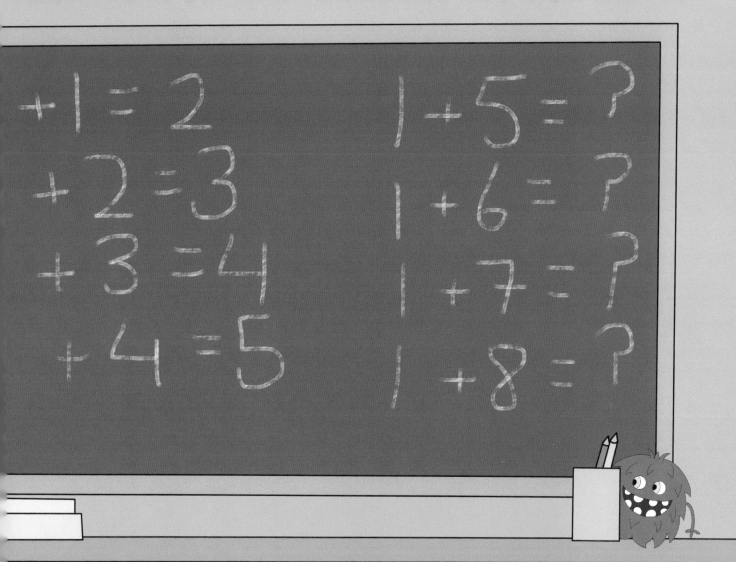

If they say no, put it down.
Being safe is always best.
Your bop will swap you something else.
Forget about the rest.

You might never see it
but trust in your bop.

It will always be there
to give you a swap.

Printed in Great Britain
by Amazon